BBC

DOCTOR WHO

THE OFFICIAL ANNUAL 2020

POLICE PUBLIC BOX

POLICE TELEPHONE
FREE FOR
USE OF PUBLIC
ADVICE & ASSISTANCE
OBTAINABLE IMMEDIATELY
OFFICERS & CARS
RESPOND TO
URGENT CALLS
PULL TO OPEN

ACCESSING TARDIS DATA FILES . . .

. . . ACCESS GRANTED

Welcome to the TARDIS Data File interface.
In this database you will find information about this Type-40
Time Travel Capsule's recent journeys and events involving its
crew. To avoid the risk of temporal paradoxes, information about
future events should *not* be accessed before they occur.

See opposite for a full listing of data files, including:

- The Space Lord Encounter
- The Riddle of Desolation
- The Judoon Incident

TDF

CONTENTS

THE SPACE LORD

It was a Mark VI combat mechanical and it had been hunting them since daybreak. The machine had pursued them through the Forest of Desolation, across the Burning Grounds, into the Valley of Agonies, and to this place. Now the chase was all but over.

The Mark VI adjusted its stealth settings and edged closer to the cave. Inside, the four humans had chosen to make their last stand. During the long pursuit, the machine had assessed each of their capabilities, finding none to be a match for its own.

It ran through their profiles now.

First, the younger male human, designation Ryan. Minimal offensive capabilities. Unarmoured. Unlike the Mark VI's active phlebotinum armour, his cellulose-based clothing provided no effective protection. Similarly, although his rubber-and-plastic shoes offered traction, they were no match for its military-grade tank tracks.

The machine accessed the next profile: the younger female human, designation Yaz. Her actions during the pursuit had demonstrated evidence of military or law-enforcement training; however, it was clear that she lacked battle experience. The Mark VI, meanwhile, had seen action across the known galaxy in the service of the Fleet before it had been drafted to the Citadel. She posed no threat.

Next, the older male human, designation Graham. Eyesight fading, bone density weak, hairline receding. He would be crushed as easily as a bugbeast of Zeta Draconis. It took a microsecond to dismiss him.

And, finally, the other female human. The Mark VI had obtained little intelligence about her during the pursuit besides the fact that she was clearly the group's leader.

Before launching the assault that would inevitably lead to their capture, the Mark VI took a moment to scan the humans one final time. Its finely tuned audio-detection circuits picked up a snatch of conversation.

'I wouldn't call it a *giant* robot,' said the female leader. 'Don't exaggerate, Graham.'

'Well, excuse me, Doc. I didn't know there was a minimum height requirement.'

The Mark VI analysed Graham's voice. The waveform suggested anxiety, along with the characteristic known as sarcasm.

'All I know,' he went on, 'is that we're being chased by a bloomin' great metal monster.'

'Actually, it's not metal,' said the woman the Mark VI now knew to be designated Doc. 'The shell is some kind of composite material. Ray-shielded, but not invulnerable. Anyway, I've seen everything I need to. That's enough running around for one day.'

'What are you talking about?' said Graham.

'You planned this, didn't you?' said Ryan. 'I knew it!'

'You mean I didn't have to knacker myself running all over this planet?' Graham protested.

'How else was I supposed to figure out what we were up against?' said Doc. 'Had to give our friend a proper run-out.'

The Mark VI paused. Its audio scan had detected something unexpected.

Ba-doom. Ba-doom.

Overlapping heartbeats, emanating from Doc. The machine drew the only logical conclusion: she had two hearts. It made the necessary correction to the profiles. Three humans. One unknown.

Identify.

The Mark VI connected to the Fleet network, and sent its query winging back to the Citadel's supercomputers, accessing the knowledge of 10,000 star systems. Four milliseconds later, it had an answer.

Species: Time Lord.

Origin: Gallifrey.

Designation: The Doctor.

A list of the most dangerous species in the universe scrolled across the Mark VI's display: Sontarans, Cybermen, the Daleks of Skaro. According to the database, they had all fallen to this Doctor's sword. Not that the machine could actually identify a sword – or indeed any kind of weapon at all – on her person.

The Mark VI hesitated.

Until that moment, every factor had pointed to an overwhelming victory in its favour, but this new information prompted it to inject a note of caution into its plan. Rather than risk close combat with a being so obviously lethal, the machine adjusted its tactics, choosing instead to launch a ranged attack. Selecting its primary armament – a plasma-beam rifle built into its right arm – the Mark VI activated the laser range-finder and calculated a firing solution.

'No good,' said Yaz, returning from the back of the cave. 'It's a dead end.' She pointed to the cave's mouth. 'That's our only way out.'

'Are you sure that robot thing's even still out there?' asked Ryan, squinting into the fast-fading daylight. 'Maybe we gave it the slip.'

With a noise like a great gulp, the interior of the cave suddenly bloomed the colour of storm-light. The air sizzled and a burning smell filled the small space, as Ryan scrambled frantically towards the back of the cave. Looking over his shoulder, he saw the boulder he had been sheltering behind was split cleanly down the middle, as neatly sliced as a loaf of bread.

'And I suppose that isn't a death ray,' grumbled Graham, brushing stone fragments out of his hair.

'Oh, that's definitely a death ray.' The Doctor grinned.

Ryan and Yaz shared a look.

'I've seen that grin before,' Ryan whispered. 'On Proxima Ceti, just before she outwitted those carnivorous chessmen.'

Yaz nodded. 'And on that derelict space station, when she worked out how to defuse the temporal anomaly bomb with three seconds left on the countdown.'

'Couldn't have done it without you,' the Doctor said, striding past them.

Ryan hadn't travelled with the Doctor for long, but even in their short time together he had seen her make impossible escapes more times than Harry Houdini – and one time he'd even seen her escape from Houdini. Well, not the real Houdini, but 200 evil cyborg clones of the great escapologist in the subways of New York City in 1904. But that was another story. What, he wondered as he watched her march towards the cave entrance, could she possibly have planned now?

The Doctor stopped beneath the stone arch at the cave's mouth. This planet had a short day–night cycle, and the sun was already low on the horizon. The last of its slanting rays cast a golden aura around the Doctor's silhouette. Standing there, glowing, she looked invincible – perhaps even immortal.

She raised both hands.

'We surrender!' she called out.

The Citadel rose twelve kilometres out of the Blasted Plains, a shining tower of iridanium steel. It was protected from every kind of weapon in the known galaxies – atomic, plasma, psionic and more – and from the endless buffeting of the tropospheric winds by force-field technology developed in its labs.

The builders and occupiers of this tower were the Fleet, a space-faring humanoid race who, having devastated their own world in a series of wars, were hungry to acquire new ones. The first ninety-seven levels of the Citadel were administrative offices. No one considered paperwork before embarking on a galactic war – no one, that is, except the Fleet. Above Admin lay Research and Development (levels ninety-eight through 112), Communications, Planning, Medical and, finally, at the pinnacle, the Space Lord himself.

From his throne room in the sky, the Space Lord waited for the strangers. News of their capture had come in over the network barely half a cycle earlier, and they would be brought into his presence shortly. Curious to observe their arrival, he watched through the great curved window set high above the Blasted Plains, despite the fact that he knew he was too high up to spot them at

the Citadel doors, even with the famed eyesight of his kind. From his spot here in the highest room in the tower, he could see more if he looked up than if he gazed down. Raising his head, he saw the flash of laser-welding equipment from the busy shipyards in low-orbit. The construction of three new dreadnoughts was nearing completion, and one of them would serve as his personal flagship in the upcoming attack on the dozing inhabitants of the mineral-rich Avolantis System.

Turning away from the window, he returned to his throne and surveyed the room in preparation for his audience. From the polished coal-black floor covering the area of two carrier decks to the triple-height doors fashioned from the hull of a captured Frost Pirate warship, it was a room designed to intimidate all who entered. The throne itself was unremarkable enough, crafted from the most precious metals in the galaxy and studded with jewels – what you'd expect.

It was the twin dorsal fins flanking the throne that really made an impression. More than ten metres high, they had been stripped from a pair of now-extinct megalovore sharks that once swam in the Outland Sea (also gone – boiled away during the Ice Cap Wars).

From the doors to the dais on which the throne sat ran a strip of red carpet lined with three two-metre-high glass cylinders on either side. It was only as visitors were guided along the path to kneel before the throne that they realised the true nature of the six glass cylinders. The First Space Lord of the Admiralty allowed himself a small smile of satisfaction as he recalled the many horrified reactions he had witnessed over the years. The cylinders were more than just ornaments; they were bottle prisons, collecting-jars in which he kept his vanquished enemies alive for his amusement. Souvenirs of war. The miserable prisoners were crammed in so tightly that they had barely any room to turn their heads – and, in the case of the three-headed Hydran of Polaris Alpha, no room at all.

Five of the six jars were occupied. By the end of the day the sixth would be too. The Space Lord grimaced. That woman had been a thorn in his side ever since she had showed up with her three companions in that ridiculous (but intriguing) vessel.

Casting a glance over his shoulder into the corner of the room behind him, he saw the ridiculous vessel in question. An insignificant blue box with no obvious propulsion device and no visible weaponry, it was surrounded by a team of his finest technicians. They were all stroking their chins in puzzlement. The hiss of a plasma-cutter filled the air as they made yet another attempt to penetrate the exterior. The flame of the cutter died, and its operator flipped up her mask and shook her head. Not even a scorch-mark.

It had no force field, and yet the box had resisted every attempt to gain entry. This only made the Space Lord more eager to understand its construction. The engineering specifications of its impenetrable hull would be invaluable to his navy. He intended to extract its secrets, either from the box or from its captain.

The throne-room doors swung open on silent hinges, and he turned to face her. There she stood, at the head of her squad. The Doctor.

They hardly look like special forces sent to disrupt my activities, the Space Lord thought, *but that may well be the intention.*

His enemies were numerous and clever.

The Mark VI combat mechanical that had captured the group now herded them along the processional path. Once again, the Space Lord was pleased by the reaction to his bottle-prisons. The young human male seemed particularly shaken. *How gratifying.* The Space Lord's pleasure was tempered, however, by the Doctor.

She stopped next to the Hydran's prison and tapped on the glass. 'Have you out of there in a mo,' she said, then – for no reason that the Space Lord could comprehend – she raised both thumbs.

He experienced a sensation he hadn't felt for a

very long time. It was so unusual that it took him by surprise, an uncharacteristic shudder of unease that made him glad of the presence of his elite guard. Ranks of them lined the throne room. Drawn from his most feared marine commando unit, they stood to attention in their massive powered exoskeleton suits, blast-visors covering their faces, bulky multi-barrelled rifles gripped in enhanced gloved hands.

But that was all mostly for show. The new Mark VI was the real threat: a robotic soldier, fearless, tireless, faithful and invincible. Just one could defeat an entire army of space marines. The Space Lord had five thousand of them! Soon his enemies would be crushed beneath their treads.

The prisoners were lined up before him and forced to pay their respects on their knees by the butt of a rifle. The Doctor got to her feet and took a step towards the throne. There was the instant

click-clack of many rifles being raised, but a flick of the Space Lord's finger caused his marines to lower their weapons. He shook off his earlier apprehension. What possible harm could come to him here in the Citadel, the heart of the Fleet empire and the most secure building in the galaxy? The thought that he needed protecting from her was amusing. *He* was the one who made others cower.

It was time to inform these intruders of their terrible fate. The Space Lord decided to go with his favourite speech – the one he'd given last month to the remnants of the government of Murgon III after he'd crushed their armada. The one he always gave to defeated opponents. It was a speech at once informative and gloating, calculated to torment the vanquished at their lowest ebb. He was just preparing to launch into the rather elegant opening paragraph when the Doctor spoke first.

'What are you going to do after?'

Once again, the Space Lord felt his usually supreme self-confidence waver. 'After what?'

'After today. When all of this is finished with.' She gestured around the throne room. 'Because you need to start thinking about the future. Maybe you could retrain.' She looked at Graham. 'They're always looking for bus drivers, right?'

Graham made a face. 'I think the intergalactic genocide might be a bit of a blot on his CV.'

The Space Lord slammed his fist against the arm of the throne. 'ENOUGH! I am Space Lord Draal, First Admiral of the Fleet, fourth of my line. Who are you to dare address me this way?'

'I'm the Doctor, first in the Gallifrey Under-tens Swimathon, thirteenth of my line.'

She raised her hand. In it was a device the size of a dagger, but it wasn't sharp like a blade. A crystal was embedded at one end. How had it slipped through the body scan? No matter.

It clearly was not a weapon. If it had been, she would already be dead. The Mark VI was programmed to respond immediately and with maximum force to any mortal threat to the Space Lord.

'We had a nice walk back to the Citadel with your giant robot here.'

'Hey, you said –' Graham began.

The Doctor waggled the device. 'Gave me just enough time to reprogram him with a little update.' She gestured to the Mark VI. 'What do you say, Bernard?'

With a whine of actuators, the Mark VI lumbered forward on its tracks, sending up a fine film of dust. The whole room shook as it rolled to the foot of the throne, then extended a massive arm. Each mechanical limb contained enough firepower to vaporise a battleship, but at that moment its metal hand contained something quite different: a small blue flower. The Mark VI offered it up.

'Have. A. Nice. Day.'

'See, Bernard here has a new set of orders,' the Doctor explained. 'Should you attempt to wage one more ridiculous war, you'll discover he doesn't like that – and neither do his five thousand friends.'

The Space Lord's unease was rapidly turning into panic. 'Five thou–' But, before he could finish, the throne-room doors flew off their hinges and crashed to the floor.

Dozens of Mark VI combat mechanicals poured through the gap.

The space marines were not only the bravest but the smartest troops in the Space Lord's navy. That's why, upon seeing the advancing robot horde, they instantly dropped their rifles in surrender.

Outside the throne room's enormous curved window, hundreds more Mark VIs hovered into view, using their antigrav engines to keep an electronic eye on the proceedings inside.

'Oh, yeah,' the Doctor said. 'When I said "update", what I meant was "virus". I replicated the new instructions across every Mark VI in your armoury. And I wouldn't try reprogramming them once I've gone.' She wagged a warning finger. 'Seriously, that would get messy. Fast.'

She swung round and pointed her not-dagger at the containment tubes. There was a hum, the crystal at the end glowed orange, and a moment later the glass prisons shattered. As their cages fell away, the occupants stumbled out of the wreckage and collapsed to the floor, gasping.

'Take them to the TARDIS,' instructed the Doctor. 'And put the kettle on.'

Yaz, Ryan and Graham helped the former prisoners to their feet, hooves or tentacles, and guided them towards the blue box behind the throne.

The Doctor produced a small key from a string round her neck, then strode across to the blue box and inserted the key into the lock below the door handle. The Space Lord and his technicians could only gawp as she swung the door open. In seconds, the group had passed inside, and only the Doctor remained, standing in the doorway of her vessel.

'I know that right now this feels like a change for the worse,' she said. 'But give it three generations – four, max – and you'll thank me.'

She stepped inside, and slammed the door shut behind her.

Over the years, the Space Lord had seen the knowledge of defeat in the eyes of a hundred opponents. Now, as his head drooped and he glanced at the polished floor, he saw it in his own reflection.

A strange sound filled the throne room. It was coming from the blue box. At first it reminded him of the howl of the Devil Bird, a creature he had hunted in the forests of his home world when he was a youth. Most of all, however, it sounded like the mocking laughter of the universe. The light on top of the blue box flashed, the vessel faded in and out of existence, and then it vanished forever.

WANT TO SEE WHERE THE DOCTOR AND HER FRIENDS GO NEXT?

Find out in THE SECRET IN VAULT 13 by DAVID SOLOMONS — in shops now!

THE WOMAN WHO FELL TO EARTH

SHEFFIELD, 2018

Strange things are happening in Sheffield. A mysterious tentacled creature terrorises passengers on a train; a dark, armoured figure stalks the streets; and a woman has fallen from the sky. She's called the Doctor, and she's here to help.

TZIM-SHA: Who are you?

THE DOCTOR: Yes! I am glad you asked that again! Bit of adrenaline, dash of outrage and a hint of panic – knitted my brain back together.
I know exactly who I am.
I'm the Doctor. Sorting out fair play throughout the universe. Now, please: get off this planet. While you still have a choice.

ACCESSING TARDIS DATA FILES . . .

ENTER PASSWORD
PASSWORD HINT: TIM SHAW'S SPECIES

. . . ACCESS GRANTED

VILLAIN SPOTLIGHT
TZIM-SHA

The fearsome Stenza warrior takes grisly trophies from the bodies of his victims – their teeth, which he embeds in his own face! In order to become the leader of his people, Tzim-Sha must hunt a random human – and he is not afraid to cheat, using a swarm of gathering coils to find his prey and an array of deadly gadgets like DNA bombs.

TIME TECH
SONIC SCREWDRIVER

The Doctor lost her sonic screwdriver when she was thrown out of the TARDIS after regenerating. With a little time in a workshop, a bit of Stenza technology and some Sheffield steel, she is able to build a new one with all the capabilities of the old device.

THE GHOST MONUMENT

DESOLATION, 2018

The Doctor's transmat device seems to have gone awry, and she's been teleported to deep space – along with Ryan, Graham and Yaz. Soon after, she finds herself caught up in a deadly race across the planet Desolation.

ACCESSING TARDIS DATA FILES . . .

ENTER PASSWORD
PASSWORD HINT: THE GHOST MONUMENT

. . . ACCESS GRANTED

THE DOCTOR: Oh, my beautiful Ghost Monument. Hello, you. I've missed you.

VILLAIN SPOTLIGHT
THE REMNANTS

Desolation is littered with the dangerous leftovers of the Stenza's science projects – from flesh-eating microbes in the water to killer SniperBots to these sinister sentinels. Though they look like old, discarded rags, the Remnants are alive, malevolent and telepathic, creeping up on their prey, then taunting and suffocating them.

TIME TECH
UNIVERSAL TRANSLATOR

Are you competing in an intergalactic rally? Do you need to be able to talk to aliens or keep in touch with your allies? Simply have your Muxteran medi-pod implant a universal translator in your body. It will translate whatever language you are hearing into whichever language you prefer!

ROSA

Having regained the TARDIS, the Doctor tries to take her friends home. However, after a few false starts, they find themselves in Alabama in the 1950s, where they must foil a villain who wants to change history for the worse . . .

ACCESSING TARDIS DATA FILES . . .

ENTER PASSWORD
PASSWORD HINT: FUTURE CRIMINAL

. . . ACCESS GRANTED

JAMES BLAKE: Y'all better make it light on yourselves and let me have those seats. Stand up now.

ROSA: I don't think I should have to.

JAMES BLAKE: Are you going to stand up?

ROSA: No.

JAMES BLAKE: If you don't stand, I'm going to have you arrested.

ROSA: You may do that.

KRASKO

Krasko is an infamous mass murderer from the far future, who has served his sentence in the Stormcage Containment Facility and been released. Though a brain implant means that he cannot directly harm anyone, he intends to use time travel and gadgets to further his racist hatred. He seeks to rewrite history according to his own twisted beliefs.

TIME TECH
TEMPORAL DISPLACEMENT WEAPON

Krasko has brought various high-tech gadgets with him from the future, including a temporal displacement device that he plans to use on Rosa Parks. The weapon sends the target back in time – as Krasko himself finds out, when Ryan turns the tables on him.

RALLY OF THE 12 GALAXIES

8

7

6

HYPERDRIVE FAILURE! MISS A TURN.

9

10

MAKE A DETOUR TO REFUEL – GO BACK ONE SPACE.

11

24

23

22

DISCOVER A STABLE WORMHOLE – ROLL AGAIN.

25

HYPERDRIVE NAVIGATION FAILURE – GO BACK TO SQUARE 17.

26

27

Angstrom and Epzo are racing towards the planet Desolation, where they each hope to be the first to reach the fabled Ghost Monument. Can you guide them there?

This is a game for two players. You will need two counters – one for each player – and a six-sided dice.

• Roll the dice to decide who starts. Whoever rolls the highest number goes first.

• Players take turns rolling the dice and moving their counters forward the number of squares shown on the dice.

• If a player lands on a square with instructions, they must follow the instructions before finishing their turn.

• If one player lands on the same square as the other player, each player should take turns to roll the dice. The player who rolls the higher number must move one square forward, and the player who rolls the lower number must move one square back. Follow any instructions on the new squares. If the two rolls are the same, nobody moves, and the next player takes their turn.

5

4

3
SLINGSHOT AROUND
A BLACK HOLE –
ROLL AGAIN.

2

1
START
HERE

12

13
INSPECTED BY
JUDOON PATROL –
MISS A TURN.

14

15

16
SHORTCUT THROUGH
AN ASTEROID BELT – GO
FORWARD TWO SPACES.

21

20

19
ENCOUNTER A TIME
WARP – GO BACK TO THE
SPACE YOU CAME FROM.

18

17

28

29
INTERCEPT A TRANSMAT
BEAM – SWAP PLACES
WITH THE OTHER PLAYER.

30

31
HIT BY SPACE
DEBRIS – GO BACK
THREE SPACES.

32

YOU
WIN!

35

34

33

POLICE PUBLIC BOX

ARACHNIDS IN THE UK

SHEFFIELD, 2018

The TARDIS finally makes it back to Sheffield, but there's something nasty creeping around the city. What does a plague of overgrown spiders have to do with billionaire Jack Robertson and his brand-new hotel?

ACCESSING TARDIS DATA FILES . . .

ENTER PASSWORD
PASSWORD HINT: EIGHT LEGS

. . . ACCESS GRANTED

THE DOCTOR: Crisis investigators. You just ran really quickly out of a room, looking really scared. Tell me exactly what's going on, omitting no detail, no matter how strange.

JACK ROBERTSON: A giant spider just smashed through my bathtub and took out my bodyguard, Kevin.

THE DOCTOR: Right. Very succinct summary.

Once an ordinary spider, this gigantic creature was accidentally 'disposed of' in Jack Robertson's landfill site full of toxic chemicals. The chemicals triggered a bizarre mutation that caused the spider to grow to a colossal size – a transformation which was killing it, as its lungs were unable to work properly in such a large body.

TIME TECH
SPIDER REPELLENT

The Doctor is never afraid to use a low-tech solution when it's the best one available. A strong-smelling mixture of vinegar and garlic paste, found in many home kitchens, is an effective barrier against spiders, which 'smell' through their feet – even giant ones.

THE TSURANGA CONUNDRUM

TSURANGAN MEDICAL TRANSPORT, SIXTY-SEVENTH CENTURY

The Doctor and her friends find themselves in need of medical attention, and luckily a hospital ship is nearby to help. But something impossibly deadly has found its way on board as well, and everyone's lives are at risk.

ACCESSING TARDIS DATA FILES . . .

ENTER PASSWORD
PASSWORD HINT: PILOT

. . . ACCESS GRANTED

YAZ: I am really trusting you on this bomb, but I don't know what you're doing –

THE DOCTOR: Think of the Pting as a mouse. And the bomb as a piece of cheese.

YAZ: A very large piece of cheese about to explode and take us all with it.

THE DOCTOR: It's not a perfect analogy, I'll admit.

VILLAIN SPOTLIGHT
PTING

The Pting is one of the universe's strangest and most feared creatures. It may be small and harmless-looking, but the Pting is indestructible, ravenously hungry and able to devour anything in its search for energy. A Pting on a starship will simply eat its way to – and through – the engines, as well as eating anything that gets in its way.

TIME TECH
ANTI-MATTER DRIVE

The *Tsuranga* is powered by an anti-matter engine: a particle accelerator that creates anti-particles, which are then annihilated to produce energy. The engine casing also contains a powerful bomb, in case the ship becomes dangerously infected and has to be destroyed.

DEMONS OF THE PUNJAB

PUNJAB, 1947

RYAN: Who's doing this stuff?

PREM: Ordinary people who've lived here all their lives. Whipped into a frenzy, to be part of a mob. Nothing worse than when normal people lose their minds.

Yaz asks to see something of her grandmother Umbreen's past, and the Doctor agrees to take her back to her roots. When they arrive in the Punjab, 1947, they discover a mysterious alien presence – and other, more human, evils.

ACCESSING TARDIS DATA FILES . . .

ENTER PASSWORD
PASSWORD HINT: YASMIN'S GRANDMOTHER

. . . ACCESS GRANTED

The Thijarians were a race that had evolved to become the universe's most deadly assassins, but when their planet, Thijar, was destroyed, the last of this ancient people gave up the art of killing. They now travel through space and time, bearing witness to and honouring those who would otherwise have died alone and unmourned.

The Thijarians make heavy use of transmat technology – that is, matter transmission – which allows them to teleport people from one place to another, including to and from their ship. The Doctor is able to block their use of this technology using transmat locks.

CATCH 22

Can you find all 22 of the Thirteenth Doctor's friends, enemies and locations in the grid below?

```
V J G G C R O S A P A R K S F
O W N A H K N I M S A Y L Z G
S N A I R A J I H T G A H I H
A Z G H C L S N T U R E P Z O
N Z C N S T A C K O A P S A S
G L A I E M A D X C H A N G T
S O S N W R I A M S A Q I N M
T G Z O T P R T A N M H P A O
O R A N I K O P F L O O C E N
O I L I M S M J B C B G R U U
M O L G T P A V R E R M B S M
S R E D I P S R E R I E O T E
B N E E R B M U K W E L T V N
S H E F F I E L D K N F S E T
E J S E M A J G N I K V O O R
```

1	ANGSTROM	9	MORAX	17	STENZA
2	EPZO	10	PTING	18	THIJARIANS
3	GCHQ	11	RECON SCOUT	19	TIM SHAW
4	GHOST MONUMENT	12	ROSA PARKS	20	TSURANGA
5	GRAHAM O'BRIEN	13	SHEFFIELD	21	UMBREEN
6	KERBLAM	14	SNIPERBOTS	22	YASMIN
7	KING JAMES	15	SOLITRACT		KHAN
8	KRASKO	16	SPIDERS		

THE PTING
DILEMMA

The Pting is one of the most dangerous creatures in the universe – and it looks surprisingly adorable! In fact, it is almost identical to the unrelated Fward species, which looks just as adorable, but is completely harmless.

LUCKILY, THE FWARD ALWAYS TRAVEL IN IDENTICAL PAIRS. CAN YOU TELL WHICH OF THESE CREATURES IS REALLY A PTING?

A

B

C

D

E

F

G

KERBLAM!

MOON OF KANDOKA

Everybody loves Kerblam! The intergalactic retailer delivers whatever you want, whenever you want it, to wherever you are – even if you're in a TARDIS. The Doctor's latest package, though, has an unexpected addition: a note that reads 'HELP ME'.

ACCESSING TARDIS DATA FILES . . .

ENTER PASSWORD
PASSWORD HINT: PROTOTYPE DROID

. . . ACCESS GRANTED

THE DOCTOR: Don't like bullies, don't like conspiracies, don't like people being in danger. And there's a flavour of all three here. Now, ever hidden in a panelled alcove?

YAZ: No.

RYAN: No.

THE DOCTOR: You haven't lived.

When you order something from Kerblam, it is delivered by one of the company's small army of teleporting robots – the Kerblam Men. Back on the moon of Kandoka, more Kerblam TeamMates keep the operation running smoothly. The Kerblam Men are your friends – at least, as long as nothing has gone wrong with the system . . .

TIME TECH
BUBBLE WRAP

Every delivery from Kerblam is carefully packed in bubble wrap, to make sure your order gets to you in perfect condition. But Charlie Duffy modified the bubble wrap so that it contains powerful explosives – just by popping a bubble, a shockwave is released that vaporises anyone in the area.

THE WITCHFINDERS

BILEHURST CRAGG, LANCASHIRE, EARLY SEVENTEENTH CENTURY

The Doctor wants to take her friends to see Elizabeth I being crowned, but instead they find themselves caught up in a witch-hunt. Terrible things are stirring at Bilehurst Cragg – can the Doctor discover its secret, with a little help from King James?

BECKA SAVAGE: Do you know why the ducking-stool was invented, Doctor? To silence foolish women who talked too much.

THE DOCTOR: Yeah, I did know that. Which is daft, because talking's brilliant. Like, if you talk to me now, I can help.

ACCESSING TARDIS DATA FILES . . .

ENTER PASSWORD
PASSWORD HINT: MISTRESS BECKA'S SURNAME

. . . ACCESS GRANTED

THE MORAX

The hideous Morax are a race of mud-like aliens, whose tendrils are able to infect and puppet other lifeforms, and even animate the dead. Billions of years ago, they were sentenced to imprisonment for war crimes and buried in Pendle Hill, where a locking mechanism in the shape of a tree kept them from escaping – until the tree was cut down.

MORAX PRISON

Pendle Hill is, in fact, a highly advanced prison. The Morax are reduced to their DNA for mass storage and locked in using a biometric system disguised as a 'sacred tree'. The wood of the tree is deadly to the Morax, causing them to burst into flame.

IT TAKES YOU AWAY

NORWAY, 2018

A dilapidated cabin in the Norwegian woods; a blind girl whose father is missing; and something terrifying roaming the forest. The Doctor must discover the truth of what is happening, but it will astonish even her . . .

THE SOLITRACT: I miss you. I miss it all so much.

THE DOCTOR: I know. But if you do this, I promise, you and I will be friends forever. You have to let me go.

THE SOLITRACT: I will dream of you out there, without me.

ACCESSING TARDIS DATA FILES . . .

ENTER PASSWORD
PASSWORD HINT: THE MIRROR

. . . ACCESS GRANTED

The Antizone is a mysterious buffer dimension existing between our reality and the mirror realm created by the Solitract. Its inhabitants include Ribbons – an untrustworthy, troll-like creature who makes his home there – and the hideous Flesh Moths, a ravenous swarm of killer insects that can devour a person in seconds.

TIME TECH
MIRROR PORTAL

The portal between our universe and the Antizone is disguised as an ordinary mirror – except that it doesn't reflect things in the usual way. Passing through the mirror and the Antizone leads to the Solitract's mirror realm, where everything is subtly reversed.

SURVIVE THE ANTIZONE

The Antizone is a weird and cavernous pocket dimension between two universes, and it is filled with strange creatures. A portal at one end leads to our universe, and a portal at the other end leads to the universe created by the Solitract. Can you lead the Doctor's friends to safety through the caverns, avoiding the ravenous Flesh Moths and the cunning Ribbons?

START

END

MIRROR, MIRROR

When the Doctor and her friends go through the looking-glass into the Solitract's universe, everything is reversed in small ways. Can you spot six differences between these pictures?

39

THE *BATTLE OF RANSKOOR AV KOLOS*

RANSKOOR AV KOLOS, 2018

The TARDIS has received nine distress calls from one planet – the planet Ranskoor Av Kolos. A terrible battle has been fought there, and the Doctor is about to discover an old enemy – with a monstrous plan for revenge on the galaxy.

THE DOCTOR: Nine cries for help, nine distress signals, all coming from the same planet. Planet of Ranskoor Av Kolos.

YAZ: Ranskoor Av what?

THE DOCTOR: Kolos. Roughly translated means 'Disintegrator of the Soul'.

GRAHAM: Oh, another cheery one.

VILLAIN SPOTLIGHT
SNIPERBOTS

Tzim-Sha's SniperBots are remorseless robotic killing machines. Armed with laser rifles, they can overwhelm their enemies with the sheer force of their numbers, but they are not very intelligent. A clever opponent can use this to their tactical advantage, and manoeuvre the SniperBots into disastrous 'friendly fire' incidents.

TIME TECH
STASIS CHAMBER

Using Stenza technology, and the astonishing reality-warping power of the Ux, Tzim-Sha is able to snatch entire planets out of space, destroying all life on the surface. The planets are then miniaturised and stored inside stasis chambers to be kept as grisly trophies.

ACCESSING TARDIS DATA FILES . . .

ENTER PASSWORD
PASSWORD HINT: TROPHY-TAKER

. . . ACCESS GRANTED

RESOLUTION

SHEFFIELD, 2019

Something sinister has been buried for centuries beneath Sheffield Town Hall – an ancient enemy that humanity once thought it had defeated. When archaeologists unearth the enemy, and unwittingly restore it to life, the Doctor must face the Daleks once again.

ACCESSING TARDIS DATA FILES . . .

ENTER PASSWORD
PASSWORD HINT: OLD ENEMY

. . . ACCESS GRANTED

DALEK: Who are you? Identify!

THE DOCTOR: Oh, mate. I'm the Doctor. Ring any bells?

DALEK: The Doctor is an enemy of all Daleks! Exterminate!

THE DOCTOR: Yes, I am. You want this planet, you have to come through me.

Reconnaissance scout Daleks are infiltration experts, enhanced with special abilities to allow them to survive alone on alien worlds and to prepare them for invasion by the main Dalek fleet. They are capable of controlling life forms by plugging in to a life form's nervous system, and they can make severed parts of the Dalek's body teleport back together.

TIME TECH
HOME-MADE DALEK SHELL

The Dalek mutant that is controlling Lin forges itself a new travel shell using scrap stolen from a lab that is investigating alien tech. It is just as formidable as standard Dalek casings, and even has built-in rocket launchers powerful enough to destroy a tank.

SONIC SWEEPER

A SONIC PROBE, LANCE OR SCREWDRIVER CAN BE A REMARKABLY VERSATILE TOOL. CAN YOU USE IT TO DETECT THE PRESENCE OF DEADLY SONIC MINES?

Each number in the grid below shows how many mines there are in the surrounding squares. Mines can be vertical, horizontal or diagonal to the numbered square. Squares with numbers in them have no mines, and there cannot be more than one mine per square. Can you pinpoint the location of each mine?

	2		2		2			1	1
1		3	4	2	3		3		1
1	3		3			1		2	1
	3			2	3			2	
2		4	4	4			2		
	4					4			1
2	5			5			3	3	2
	4		5						
2				2		2	4	3	3
	3		3				2		1

TIME LORD MATRIX

The Doctor's exploits are recorded in the Time Lord Matrix on Gallifrey — a remarkable database linked to every TARDIS in existence. Can you fit the code names of these adventures into the Matrix network?

4-letter word
ROSA

7-letter word
KERBLAM

12-letter word
WITCHFINDERS

13-letter word
GHOST MONUMENT

14-letter word
IT TAKES YOU AWAY

15-letter word
RANSKOOR AV KOLOS

16-letter word
ARACHNIDS IN THE UK

17-letter words
DEMONS OF THE PUNJAB

TSURANGA CONUNDRUM

19-letter word
WOMAN WHO FELL TO EARTH

THE RHINO OF TWENTY-THREE STRAND STREET

'There's a rhino in Mrs McCarthy's garden.'

Patricia Kiernan didn't say it because she thought anyone was listening; people didn't listen to Patricia, as a rule.

There were two reasons for this. The first was that, while her father always announced the fact he was about to speak by snorting manfully and clearing his nasal passages like a dedicated player of the tuba, Patricia didn't start conversations because she'd never finished one. She'd begun talking at six months old and continued pretty much without interruption, a constant stream of observations, ideas and facts that washed around the Kiernan home like the background hum of a radiator – sometimes welcome but mostly ignored.

The second reason was that Patricia was ten.

'There's a rhino in Mrs McCarthy's garden,' she said again. The snow was coming down thick and fast outside, and her mam was darting between saucepans and her brother was begging Dad for a go of the record player and there was a rhino snuffling at Mrs McCarthy's holly wreath. Holly was poisonous – Patricia had read that. Mrs McCarthy had a bush in her back garden. Dad had been trying to convince Mrs McCarthy to get rid of it, but then she'd gone and died, which Dad said was exactly the kind of thing the woman would do just to win an argument.

It hadn't been holly that had killed Mrs McCarthy. She'd been old – very old, so wrinkled that her eyes disappeared fully when she smiled, which was pretty much constantly. She would have smiled at seeing the rhino, Patricia thought. Patricia had grown up in Mrs McCarthy's shabby living room as much as in her own house, and had once heard the old lady say that she loved surprises at Christmas, 'but the more Christmases you see, the harder surprise is to find'.

The rhino, Patricia felt, would have qualified.

Rhinos lived on the African savannah, which was hot and flat and not quite a desert, and they lived in Sumatra and India and Java. They were megafauna, which meant they were not just animals but large animals, sometimes up to a ton in weight, and they were endangered because some people thought their horns were magic, which further darkened Patricia's already low opinion of magic.

(Patricia did not believe in magic, or wizards, or fate. She did believe everything happened for a reason, but she believed that reason was physics.)

There were only a few rhinos left, and they said that by the year 2000 there might be none. Patricia knew there were only a few places in the world where you could find rhinos, and nothing in any of the books she had read said that one of those places was a back garden in an Irish suburb a week before Christmas in 1966 – but, by the looks of it, this rhino didn't seem to mind.

'Dinner,' her mother said, and Patricia automatically clambered into position. The Kiernan house was so small that the chairs had to be pulled out from under the table in a specific order or nobody could get in from the living room, and Patricia, being the smallest, had to scramble round everyone else so that the system would work.

By the time she managed to get back to the window, the rhino was gone.

The nuns didn't teach zoology at Lakelands Convent School. It wasn't something girls needed. Girls needed language classes. They needed sewing lessons. They needed religion most of all, according to the Mother Superior, because sins were always waiting – legions of them, hidden like trapdoors in everyday life. There was a long list of sins, read out every morning at Mass. Some of them Patricia had to look up.

But the children who attended that grim, cabbagey-smelling school had developed an interest in zoology all the same, because it was essential when it came to dealing with nuns. The nuns wafted down the corridors, stark and white and terrifying as swans, all with different predilections (a word that meant habits).

There was Sister Jacinta's halitosis (a word that meant bad breath), Sister Miriam's inhuman aim with bits of chalk and Sister Victoria's tradition of telling the girls which of them she thought did and didn't have futures. When it came to surprise megafauna, however, there was only really one nun you could ask.

'Sister Agnes, what do you know about rhinos?'

Sister Agnes was stout and small, her face flushed as a new apple. There was a stretched shininess to her cheeks, as if they were unable to keep all that personality inside. 'I wager,' she said, with the lilting Cork accent that made every sentence a poem, 'less than you, Miss Kiernan. You've read all of our books on animals, I believe.'

Bragging was a sin.

'Yes, Sister Agnes.'

'And you still have questions?'

'Yes, Sister. Just a couple, Sister.'

'Well, the Lord admires an inquisitive mind,' Sister Agnes said, which to Patricia seemed to directly contradict quite a few of the Mother Superior's sermons, but maybe nuns were allowed to disagree.

She forged ahead. 'Rhinos live in the savannah, don't they?'

'I believe so,' Sister Agnes said. 'In Africa, anyway. I'm not sure of the exact address.'

This was a joke.

'And there haven't been any . . .'

'Any what?'

Escaped zoo rhinos. Rhino exchange programmes. Rhino sanctuaries in Ringsend. Lying was a sin, and so was keeping secrets, but until Patricia knew exactly what she was supposed to be saying, until she knew exactly what the situation was, telling anyone would also be lying.

Sister Victoria looked at the kids like she knew every bad word they'd ever said. The Mother Superior's stare could strip paint. But Sister Agnes looked as if she couldn't just see the thoughts inside children's heads but, uniquely for a nun, as if she understood them too.

'Patricia?'

'Nothing, Sister. Never mind.'

***

She took the long way home, skirting Sandymount Strand where Dublin fell away into the iron-grey sea, and the skeletal, fenced-off construction site where the Poolbeg towers were promised to rise, and everywhere she could she collected plants; colt's foot and yellow Alexander and wiry strands of beach reeds, until her bag was bulging with yellow and green. Rhinos ate almost constantly, and pickings were slim in Dublin in December, so she took everything she could. Maybe beach reeds were delicious to rhinos? She hadn't been able to find a definitive answer in any of her books. This was what Patricia's burgeoning scientific sensibilities thought of as the 'experimental' phase.

The last ingredient came from her kitchen, and for once Patricia was glad of being invisible – skinny and pale, just a slip of a thing with a crescent fringe and a gap in her smile. Technically she knew the satsumas in the kitchen were for their Christmas stockings, so she only took one and assumed the other would go to her brother, and then she was back out on the street.

It wasn't breaking in, Patricia told herself to quiet the nun in her head. She had her mother's key, orphaned from the fat set in the hall because Mam didn't quite know what to do with it and got a little weepy when Dad asked. Mrs McCarthy didn't have any family. What happened to houses

when nobody was there to claim them?

The house itself looked unworried about its precarious future – just another one-storey cottage huddling up against the others on the street. That didn't sit right with Patricia's ordered mind. She knew that physics meant that the world was always changing, even if we didn't see it, but the house looked exactly as it had when Mrs McCarthy was alive.

It felt disrespectful.

Patricia took a deep breath, opened the gate and stepped up to the door.

That was when everything changed.

Something swept over her, scudding and popping along her skin as if she'd just stepped through a soap bubble. It tickled like the precious cans of fizzy orange they were allowed on special occasions. Her ears went *gloing gloing*, the way they did when she was swimming, and all sound from the city outside seemed to stop.

It wasn't scary. That was her first thought. It didn't hurt and wasn't like anything she'd ever felt before, so she wasn't at all frightened by it. It was just . . . odd.

But then she looked up at the house, and *then* she was frightened, because something had come down through Mrs McCarthy's roof like a foot through a doll's house. It had torn a hole wider than she was tall, and impacted so hard that slates had popped free from the roof and cracks had spread down through the walls.

The whole house looked *squeezed*, the brick puckering out a little the way cheese did in a sandwich that had been in her bag all day.

Slowly and carefully, Patricia backtracked through the bubble. Standing in the street, Mrs McCarthy's looked completely normal. No hole, no cracks. Standing in the street, she could hear cars and birds and Aunt Carol (who hated the Brits and put brown sauce in her tea).

She stepped into the bubble again – *Pop! Fizz!* – and spent a couple of minutes taking down notes in her copybook.

> There is a bubble round Mrs McCarthy's house.
> It is hiding what is inside. It is showing a different version of the house. Like TV.
> There's snow on the house when you're inside the bubble. No snow when you're outside it. Maybe the image is old?
> The image is hiding a hole in the roof.
> The sides of the hole are all glassy and burnt, like the thing that broke in was hot.

She took notes because that was what scientists did, and not because she was trying to work up the nerve to go through the door. That was the other thing scientists did: they discovered. A scientist would go into the house.

Mrs McCarthy's hallway was at once exactly and nothing like the way she remembered it.

The pictures of Jesus and the Pope and Padre Pio were still all present, but they'd hopped off their frames. Huge cracks ran down the walls. The carpet was all churned and torn. It even smelled different – the warm apple smell that had always been there was squeezed out, along with the architecture, to make way for a muskier, earthier smell. It wasn't bad, exactly, just *big* – a smell she had to breathe around rather than through.

The rhino was in the sitting room.

It was definitely a rhino, now that she could see it up close. Nothing else had that huge slab of head, those strangely delicate, flicking ears, and nothing else had that horn – that magic horn, the horn that got them into trouble. She could tell it was a rhino, though its arms and legs seemed almost human-long, wrapped in some kind of silvery fabric, and she could tell that it was young (though its face was just as wrinkled as Mrs McCarthy's had been) and she could tell that it was sick, because it was on its side and its breath was coming in wheezing gasps.

'The holly,' she whispered, and then its liquid eyes rolled to her.

'No, no! Wait!' she yelped, but it had already panicked, staggering to its feet, its too-long forelimbs wrapped round its stomach. Only years of living in a small house with a large and inattentive father saved her from being crushed, because there was not a lot of room and quite a lot of rhino. It was shorter than her but far wider and, as she ducked the massive swerve of a shoulder, all she could think was that many, many more people killed rhinos than the other way round, and maybe this rhino also knew that and wasn't happy about it.

'Wait!' she said again, skidding on a pile of what had to be vomit and landing hard against the wall.

The rhino stomped into a turn, looking at her with first one eye, then the other.

'I brought food. I brought –'

A great, dragging snort then that would have reminded her of her father had she not been so afraid. It wasn't even up to her shoulder, but it was nearly as wide as her dad, and terribly, terribly strong. Most of Mrs McCarthy's furniture had been smashed to flinders and arranged in some kind of nest, and she could see splinters sticking to its silvery covering from where it had rearranged the house around itself.

With its great head lowered, it sniffed again. *Respect.* That was what professional zoologists said: you had to respect animals and they would respect you. 'Satsuma,' she whispered, and held it up.

The rhino lurched away, spooked at the sound of her voice, and she winced as more pictures were ground under its lumpen feet. There was something strange about them, but it was hard to see with its massive head in her face.

Rhinos always looked grumpy. It was how their faces were made. They were like nuns in that respect. But when it stopped again and stared at the satsuma, glowing in her palm like a little chunk of sun in the cold December gloom, it looked hungry as well.

'Of course,' she whispered. 'You've been sick. You're probably starving. Would you like it?'

Her hand inched forward. Its head did too, and slowly, very slowly, arms still wrapped around its stomach as if in terrible pain, it turned to bite the satsuma from her palm. She felt the fruit pop, and juice suddenly baptised her fingers, sticky and sweet.

'There,' she said gently, as its throat worked. 'That's good, isn't it?'

The rhino flinched back, its eyes fixed on hers – brown as almonds, somehow bright and dark all at once . . .

Animals were smart. It was why Patricia had never asked her parents for a pet, even though she wanted one so much it was an ache in her chest. She wanted something she could love and

look after, but she lived in a little house that was cramped already and she couldn't bear the thought of letting the pet down. The Mother Superior said that people had been put above animals and it was their job to serve us, but as far as Patricia could see the only difference was that people had voices and animals didn't, and so someone had to look after them.

And fair enough, the rhino was twice her width, but it was still afraid, and just like that it was Patricia's job to make sure it wasn't any more.

Slowly, she opened the bag at her feet and tipped out all of the plants she'd collected. She didn't want to rush things. The rhino had a lot to think about, and so did she.

'I'll come back tomorrow,' she said. The rhino was caught between warily watching her and staring with undisguised longing at the greenery on the ground. 'It was nice to meet you.'

'Miss Kiernan.'

All the other girls had left. The snow flurried against the windows and Sister Agnes had her arms folded, her eyebrows in what the staffroom had already begun to call 'the Patricia position'.

'Miss Kiernan, it's lunchtime.'

Without taking her eyes from her work, the little girl withdrew a flattened cheese sandwich from her bag and took a purposeful bite.

'Patricia, I appreciate your curiosity . . .' *Though others won't*, Sister Agnes thought, *and eventually quiet little Patricia is going to get noticed.*

Some of the other sisters thought it was a waste letting the girls have a library at all. Sister Victoria, who thought herself a poet despite lacking the empathy God gave a whelk, said that there was a cruelty in it, like putting a caged bird in a place where they could see the sky. But Sister Agnes didn't think like that, because it wasn't a teacher's job to decide what was good and what was bad. It was, technically, a nun's job, but that was why she had decided a long time ago that she'd rather be a bad nun and a good teacher instead.

'Patricia, what are you doing?'

'Research.'

Unfortunately, research had provided Patricia with more questions than answers. This initially did not bother her. That was what science was all about – learning the connections, figuring out how much you didn't know.

Certain facts had proved easy. She'd learned not to bring branches because, while black rhinos had beaky lips that allowed them to eat hard things, white rhinos had soft, square mouths, and apparently Ringsend rhinos did too. She wrote in her notebook:

Are you a white rhino?

She'd learned rhinos could live up to five days without water as long as they were getting greens, but she'd filled a bath up anyway and the rhino had cautiously drank. She'd even brought a bucket of mud, being careful not to ruin her uniform, because rhinos had thin skins and liked to armour themselves with muck.

But there were . . . inconsistencies between the Ringsend rhino and the rhinos in her books; inconsistencies that the books didn't seem to be able to explain. Its silvery clothes, for one – wrapping limbs long enough that its walk was more of a primate tramp than the waddle

she'd seen in the rhinos at Dublin Zoo. It walked like a person, or nearly like a person, or more like a person than a rhino should.

And it had hands. That was the main difference. She hadn't noticed the first time she'd been there because it had been clutching its stomach, but now they dangled at the ends of its arms: thick, blunt and four-fingered, but definitely, actually hands.

'What are you?' Patricia whispered as she dumped out more grass. 'You're behind some kind of . . . hologram.' She'd picked up the word from a science-fiction show on television, which didn't feel very scientific, but it was better than nothing. She'd examined the bubble as much as she was able to without being the girl standing on the street staring at an empty house, and it seemed to just be a veil, like a painted backdrop hiding the reality underneath.

'Did you put that up? Are you . . .' She didn't want to say 'are you smart', because that seemed rude, but there were so many things here that made so little sense that she could only focus on one at a time.

Patricia had narrowed it down to three questions.

1. What are you?
2. How are you hiding the house?
3. Where are you from?

Unfortunately, the rhino wasn't talking. They had made some progress. It no longer retreated to a corner when she spoke; instead, it just sat there in the remains of Mrs McCarthy's chair, pushing reeds around the floor the way a kid might spaghetti. Once, she had patted it, and she'd thought it had nuzzled a little into her hand, but it might have just been hoping for more satsumas.

'Are you from Africa? The savannah? South Africa? Kenya?'

She was trying to be specific. Mostly because

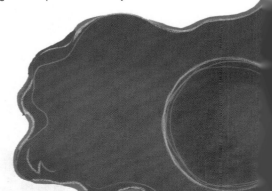

she was Patricia, but also because the nuns talked about Africa like it was a street, and they talked about 'the problems over there' like the whole continent was an aunt who kept coming over to borrow sugar. Only when she was safe behind the bubble did Patricia let herself think about the fact that she knew Africa had more than forty different countries and 2,000 languages and that if they did have problems it was probably the fault of the people who kept coming over and trying to tell them what to do.

A little part of Patricia understood that at some point she was probably going to get into trouble. Not because of the rhino – though yes, maybe – but just for being Patricia. She was small and she was well behaved, but sometimes she could feel the things she read filling her up and making her bigger, and eventually, like a rhino in a living room, something would get broken. It was a lonely feeling.

Maybe that was why she talked to the rhino so much.

Patricia wasn't surprised the rhino was a little standoffish. She had trouble understanding the people around her, and they were the same species. This creature – this shambling riddle with its almost-human form and huge, animal head – must have felt even lonelier than she did.

'Where are you from? Did you do this bubble thing? Do you know where you are now?'

One of those lumpish, thick hands reached

down and picked up a reed, and then tipped over the pail of mud. Patricia yelped, jumping backwards as gritty water splashed over her uniform, staining the pristine white a dark and dirty grey. Her cheeks burned red; Mam had enough washing to do, and her dad would be so angry and –

The rhino just stared at the floor, the reed still clutched in its hand.

'Why did you do that?' she snapped. 'I'm already in trouble for getting caught stealing Mr Reilly's tulip bulbs, which I did for you, and now I . . . I . . .'

The reed scratched its way across the drying mud, as if the animal was ashamed, and Patricia trailed off, feeling abruptly bad. And then she realised. It wasn't ashamed. It was drawing.

Circle after circle after circle. Nine in all, some small and some big, and for a second Patricia thought it was writing in some sort of language, even though of *course* that was silly. It stared at her with its deep-set eyes, then ended the row of circles with a curved line so large it could have swallowed all the others, and that was when Patricia realised the truth was far more ridiculous.

Nine circles, then a huge one.

Deliberately, the rhino stabbed the third circle along.

Do you know where you are now?

It was answering her question.

The circles were the planets of the solar system. It was pointing at Earth.

It was time to tell a nun.

Rhinos were one thing. Rhinos with hands and clever, wounded eyes were another. But a rhino with hands and clever, wounded eyes who knew where it was in the solar system and was hiding behind what Patricia thought might be a hologram?

Sister Agnes would know what to do.

She'd thought about telling her parents, but she was afraid her dad would laugh at her the way he had when she'd asked him for a Young Scientist Kit!™. Mam had said she couldn't have one because they were saving to send her brother to technical school, but that didn't explain to Patricia at all why her wanting a science kit would be funny.

No. It had to be Sister Agnes.

Patricia pushed open the school's thick glass doors, for once not wrinkling her nose at the cabbage smell. It was after school, but most of the nuns lived at Lakelands as well as taught there, and sometimes there were meetings in the evening, presumably about sin.

Sister Agnes wasn't in her room. There was nobody in the staffroom either. Wandering the corridors, Patricia began to confront the fact that maybe her classmate Maebh hadn't been wrong about the nuns hanging upside down to sleep in the closets like bats. Finally, out of sheer desperation, she climbed the cold stone stairs to the Mother Superior's office, hoping she might meet Sister Agnes on the way.

Voices were drifting down the stairwell.

'I really don't see what the problem is.'

Sister Agnes. Patricia froze, her hand on the banister.

'The problem, *Sister*, is that she will get herself into trouble. The smart ones always do.'

There was an arch and terrible fury to the Mother Superior's voice, an arctic, ever-present wrath at the world and all its failures, whether she was addressing 200 frightened girls or thanking the postman. It was why, despite every Sunday sermon, Patricia imagined hell as cold instead of hot.

'That's not –'

'It is, Agnes. You know it is. We've seen it time and time again. I already have her father on to me, saying that we're giving her notions with all these books. It's a disservice to her. Sister Victoria is right – songbirds shouldn't look at the sky. You'll leave her discontented with her lot, and you know where that leads.'

'Miss Kiernan is a very bright girl!'

Patricia went cold.

'That's the problem,' the Mother Superior said icily. 'All those books. Botany. Zoology. *Physics.* These are not the things with which a girl should be concerning herself. She's been going around taking flower cuttings. Did you know that? Making a nuisance of herself. She doesn't know her place, Agnes. And girls who don't know their place get themselves into trouble.'

'I just want her to be herself.'

'Why?'

A gasp. A tiny, shocked intake of breath.

'This is what happens, Agnes. We are not raising little girls to be bright. Bright girls get noticed. Bright girls get into trouble. Bright girls get taken away. There are institutions up and down the country full of bright girls, Agnes, and no one will appreciate bright little Patricia Kiernan. I can already see it. The way the other girls think of her –'

Patricia's cheeks were burning. There was a prickling in her eyes. Her heart was hammering so hard in her chest that she was afraid the nuns would hear it. She'd never really paid any attention to the other girls – they were confusing, and books were not. She'd never thought about whether they were paying attention to her.

The Mother Superior had laid her little life out so neatly, like a mouse for dissection, and Patricia just stood there listening, a tiny thing underfoot.

There was another list in her head. One she felt bad for keeping, but she did. All the jokes her dad made. The way her stomach felt when they talked about her brother going on to college – *college*, when he had only gone to school because otherwise the nuns would come looking for him – and about Patricia getting married. Not married to anyone, just married, like someone handing off a parcel.

And, underneath it all, the sudden fear. *Bright girls get taken away.* It happened. She knew it did, though the what and where was kept from her, and that just frightened her more. Mam and Aunt Carol talked about it sometimes,

and sometimes they were angry about it and sometimes they were afraid too.

Sister Agnes's voice was subdued. 'I just wanted to give her a chance to not end up at the kitchen sink.'

'But that is where she's heading,' the Mother Superior said, and now her voice was gentle. 'The sooner she realises that, the better.'

Patricia had read thirty-three books where children ran away. She could recite the formula like a gospel. You went to bed dressed, and carried your shoes so nobody could hear you. You packed a torch, and sandwiches, and maybe a flask of tea, and just before you slipped out of the door you turned round and whispered 'Goodnight' to your family, because it was poignant.

Patricia did none of those things, because she shared a room with her brother and he would have noticed her being dressed in bed, and had she touched the food in the kitchen her mam would have said, 'Was your dinner not enough?' and she didn't stop at her doorway to turn round and be poignant because – and this made her blink tears from her eyes – her dad would consider poignancy 'notions' (a word that meant airs and graces, and was very close to a mortal sin).

Instead, she just did what she assumed normal runaways did, which was hide awake and terrified behind her closed eyelids until 2 a.m., and then she got up to go to the bathroom and didn't come back. Her schoolbag was by the door, and she threw a coat on over her pyjamas and put a whole bag of satsumas into her pockets and then she ghosted out of the door.

Running away at Christmas should have been especially poignant, but in reality it was just cold. Thinking of that supposedly special day with Mass and lectures and getting an itchy dress instead of a science kit just made Patricia feel colder.

The night and the snow combined in a strange alchemy, turning the street she knew into something completely different: bigger, the spaces between the houses deeper, the streetlights only seeming to darken the darkness to a cold and vicious black.

The now-familiar fizz washed over her, and for a moment she thought that they could just stay there, living in a different-but-the-same world. But rhinos were hungry and she'd have to forage, and eventually someone would come to claim the house.

Too big. Too bright. Neither one of them fit the world any more.

'We're going to leave,' she said as soon as she entered the sitting room. The rhino eyed her suspiciously, until she withdrew a satsuma from her pocket, and then its look turned to suspicious hunger. 'Do you understand?'

Zoologists and respect, and it was the same in the books Patricia had read about girls befriending animals too. Usually by now there was supposed to be a bond between them, a kind of mutual respect, but so far all the rhino seemed to respect was the fact that she could produce satsumas. She'd brought it paper and pens in case it wanted to draw again, and even an encyclopaedia so it could learn about the world, but it hadn't so much as cracked the spine. She hadn't even got to fall asleep against its side or have a moment of shared danger or anything.

That was fine by her. Patricia was beginning to realise she preferred non-fiction.

'I've brought my dad's coat –' which was *not* revenge for his jokes, obviously – 'and I've made a list of hiding places. We can use one a night, until we get out of Dublin.'

The rhino sniffed, and turned away, folding its arms.

'We can't stay *here*,' she said. 'Neither of us. You have to listen.'

It just stared at the wall, and Patricia felt the anger building, buoyed up by all the knowledge inside her, the secret fact lurking underneath everything she had learned: that the world was unfair, and just physics, and all she had to do to fit into it was stop being herself.

She could just say her prayers, and be good, and not get into trouble; so far looking after an ungrateful rhino had just got her scratched and muddy and looked down on, and wasn't she only going to end up at the kitchen sink anyway?

But that is where she's heading.

The Mother Superior's words wrapped round her like chains, like the bars of a cage, and she looked up to stop the tears from falling out. The hole in the roof was still there, the stars glittering beyond, and the rhino was staring up at them too – a trapped little thing looking at the sky.

The words sank through Patricia and, like a meteor entering the atmosphere, caught fire and came apart. Sometimes you didn't have to give respect to get it. Sometimes it had to be took.

'No,' she said, and the rhino's ears pricked up. 'We're not giving up. We're not staying here. The world is . . . the world is changing all the –'

There was a knock at the door.

A chill burned through Patricia's veins, driven hard by her analytical heart. It wasn't the thought of the Gardaí. It wasn't the thought of nuns. It was the sudden and scientific knowledge that for someone to have knocked on the door they had to be inside the bubble. And they had knocked anyway. Jauntily. As if they had all the time in the world.

That scared Patricia more than anything.

'Hello?'

The voice was female, but more importantly it was English. There were different English accents. Patricia knew that from the radio. This wasn't the glacial, precise English accent she had heard from politicians – every syllable smooth and sharp like a dentist's tools – but it was English all the same. English meant police. It meant government. It meant trouble, and suddenly what *else* the Mother Superior had said sent terror down Patricia's spine.

Bright girls get taken away.

She had to assume the same went for rhinos.

Moving faster than she had ever seen, the rhino reached out and grabbed her round the waist, lifting her as if she weighed nothing at all. Patricia let out a squeak as it dropped its head and *charged*.

Glass, and noise, and confusion, and by the time the world stopped whirling Patricia realised they were outside. The rhino had flung itself – and her – through the living-room window, and now it was running – properly running, dragging her off her feet with its incredible strength. She had a bouncing, jolting moment to see Mrs McCarthy's house: the bubble was gone, its destruction revealed, and a woman was standing at the door, her face bright with shock.

A sign gleamed from the shadows behind her. It said POLICE.

'Run,' Patricia whispered. '*Run!*'

Feet pounding, hearts hammering, the girl and the rhino ran through Ringsend. They took side streets and alleys, footpaths and shortcuts, any way and anywhere they could not easily be seen. *She was English. She was police. She'll have a car.* They took the footways, slipped into the sunken cinder running track, used the sheds at the Pigeon House generating station as cover, and Patricia's heart climbed her throat every time a car flashed by.

The rhino had put her down, cantering along beside her, its head swaying from side to side, massive as the keel of a boat. Rhinos could run at thirty-five miles an hour. She'd read that. Why wasn't it leaving her behind?

'Go on,' she hissed through clenched teeth. 'I'll be fine. *Go.*'

Still it kept pace beside her, horn gleaming in the light of the stars.

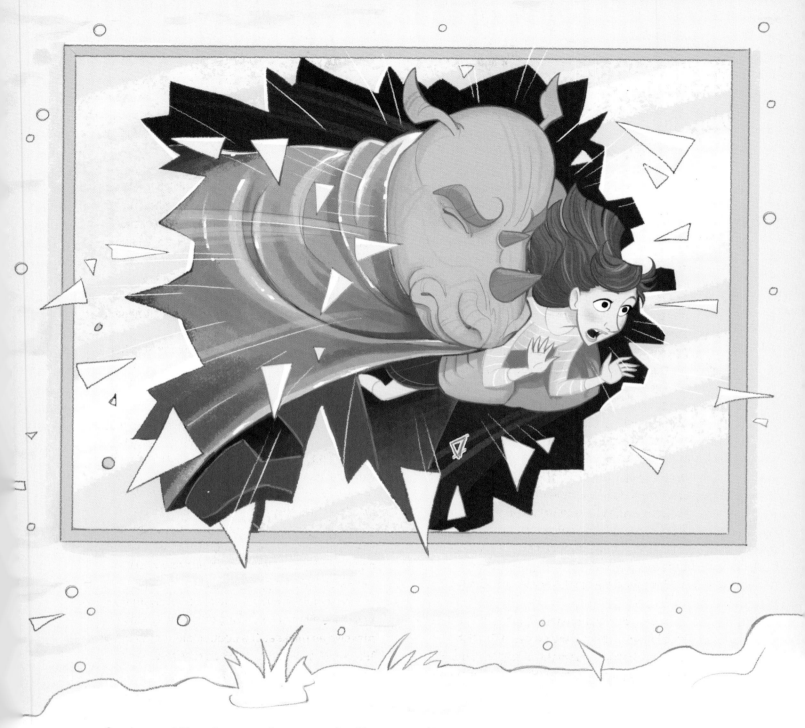

Sandymount Strand was nearly an ocean itself: a vast curve of sand, flat and featureless in beige and delicate grey. She'd never been on it at night-time before. Night-time wasn't when beaches were for, and now it looked eerie and lonely as the surface of the moon.

'The Poolbeg towers building site,' she panted. 'We get there and we can hide. I can forage for you and –'

The rhino was staring up at the stars. She couldn't blame it. Now that the city was keeping its own lights to itself, the stars glittered hugely, close enough to touch.

'Come *on*!' she shouted, and then something blew across them so fast it flung them both on to their faces. *Jet stream*, Patricia thought stupidly, sand filling her mouth and scratching her cheeks. The world swam. Her ears were popping. The rhino was wailing, and that was the sound that made her roll on to her back.

There were lights in the sky. They *moved*, separate and distinct from the stars, and the air became backwash and grit as they began to descend.

Patricia staggered to her feet, and saw a machine – a stout cylinder of steel bigger than her house. Icy wind slashed at her face, snowflakes swirling in a sun-bright beam of light that turned the night to day.

The ground shook – actually shook – as the machine landed.

A *spaceship*. The word rattled around Patricia's ribcage, trapped in orbit round her heart.

And the rhino's back went ramrod straight. Like a nun, or a teacher, it suddenly stood proud and tall, and then stumbled towards the light. Patricia recognised that run. It was the way you ran when you were little, when you didn't care about being able to make yourself stop because you knew someone was going to catch you.

A platform eased from the bottom of the ship. There was a lone figure standing on it. The figure was huge and hulking, and yet when the rhino flung itself into its arms it fell as if toppled. A head the size of a continent turned to the side, horn held aloft like a policeman in a movie holstering his gun, and then its soft cheek nuzzled down.

And the platform lifted them away.

The rhino never looked back, and Patricia's eyes were filled with tears even before the ship's take-off turned the air to dust.

Patricia Kiernan watched the ship rise slowly, jerkily, until all she could see were lights and she didn't know if it was the ship or the stars. She stayed staring upwards even when the crunch of footsteps sounded behind her.

'You missed them,' she said,

hating the quaver in her voice. 'They just left.'

'Caring,' the woman said in that odd English accent, 'is the first thing people feel silly for, and the very last thing they should.'

Sometimes it's kindness that makes the tears come. Patricia felt the first sob rise like a seesaw, and she was too small to make it stay down. That was physics. Things just happened. Believing anything else was magic, and this wasn't that sort of world.

'It just left,' she whimpered. 'I can't believe it. After everything I did.'

'The Judoon are mercenaries,' the woman said. She was blonde and had a long coat, and what Patricia had thought was the shock of seeing a rhino jump through a window was actually just her face – a wide-eyed, unashamed amazement, as constant as the ice in the Mother Superior's voice. 'You know what that word means, don't you?'

'Someone who fights for money,' Patricia said, sniffling. 'How do you know I –'

'Because you were confronted with a holo-screen and a young alien half-feral with fear and loneliness, and your response was to look after it. Because I've been alive a very long time and I've never seen a girl try to give a Judoon an encyclopaedia before. You know what words mean. The Judoon are mercenaries. Their whole culture is built around it. Cost and effect. Following the system. Doing what they're told and no more.

No compassion. No mercy. "Know your place."'

Patricia was crying again. Hard. The rhino had been grumpy and mean and had mostly cared about satsumas, and yet now it was gone and she might never touch something that big and strange and unknowable again.

'And rhinos can run at thirty-five miles an hour.'

Just for a moment, Patricia felt what it was like to be anyone else in the world listening to her.

'Wh-what?'

'Judoon can run quite a lot faster, actually, because they stand on two feet. He could have left you behind. Standard Judoon Retreat Protocol. You don't have to run the fastest – you just have to run faster than everyone else. And instead he kept pace with you.'

The woman's eyes were very bright.

'There was a fight. A big fight on a world very far from here. And his mother is all alone, and trying to do the best she can, and she had to fight but she didn't want her son caught up in it as well. So she put him in a saviour pod – a machine that would bring him to a world and hide him behind a holo-screen.'

She sighed.

'I offered to babysit, but the Judoon don't like rule-breakers, and that's a bad habit I have. So I decided to check in on the sly, but he already had someone to keep him safe.'

Patricia sniffed. 'Me.'

'You. And, despite the system, despite the way he'd been raised, despite everything his society would tell him to do, he stayed with you. Because you looked after him. And you did it well too – better than most adults, I'd imagine, if a rhino crashed into their neighbour's house.'

'R-really?'

'There are a lot of worlds,' the woman said. 'And a lot of systems. A lot of scared people making cages that keep themselves on the inside and everyone else out.'

That is where she's heading.
Notions.
Songbirds shouldn't look at the sky.
'Why, though?'

'Ignorance. Anger. Fear they'll lose what they have, that there won't be enough room. But things are bigger on the inside.' She smiled innocently. 'Trust me on that.'

Patricia was a practical child, and she knew what question to ask. 'So what do I do? When people tell me what size I'm supposed to be?'

The woman thought for a moment. 'Look them in the eye, and ask them a question.'

'What question?'

The woman looked at her, and in her eyes there was a little anger and a lot of kindness, and deep in their depths Patricia could see herself, bright and small and surrounded by stars.

'Says who?'

THIS STORY IS TAKEN FROM

TWELVE ANGELS WEEPING by DAVE RUDDEN — twelve stories featuring the scariest and strangest villains from *Doctor Who.*

TARDIS DATA FILE . . .

. . . ACCESS NEXT FILE

PARADOX WARNING
ACCESS RESTRICTED FOR TIMELINE PROTECTION

TDF

LOGOFF

That's odd – some kind of data fragment. Maybe some sort of echo from my future? See if you can work out what it means – there are passwords throughout the eleven previous data files that you could use to reconstruct the code, if you're very clever . . .

The Doctor

PUZZLE ANSWERS

PAGE 30: CATCH 22

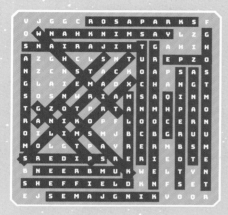

PAGE 31: THE PTING DILEMMA

E IS A PTING.

PAGE 38: SURVIVE THE ANTIZONE

PAGE 39: MIRROR, MIRROR

PAGE 44: SONIC SWEEPER

	2		2		2			1	1
1		3	4	2	3		3		1
1	3		3			1		2	1
	3			2	3			2	
2		4	4	4			2		
	4					4			1
2	5			5			3	3	2
	4		4	5					
2				2		2	4	3	3
	3		3			2		1

PAGE 45: TIME LORD MATRIX

```
        D       R
I T T A K E S Y O U A W A Y
        M       S               T
R A N S K O O R A V K O L O S   S
        N               K       U
        S           K E         R
        O           E           A
W I T C H F I N D E R S         N
        T           R   B       G
W O M A N W H O F E L L T O E A R T H
        E           B   A       C
        P           A   M       O
        U               B       N
A R A C H N I D S I N T H E U K U
        J                       N
        A                       D
        B       G H O S T M O N U M E N T
                                M
```

61